# Diwali
### in my
# NEW HOME

by Shachi Kaushik
Illustrated by Aishwarya Tandon

beaming — be

To the Round Rock Public Library—where it all started. To Anshul, my husband, for all his support and encouragement. And to my family—whom I miss being with every Diwali. —SK

To Mummy, Papa, Bhaiya, and Uncle —AT

Published in 2022 by Beaming Books, an imprint of 1517 Media. All rights reserved. No part of this book may be reproduced without the written permission of the publisher. Email copyright@1517.media. Printed in Canada.

28  27  26  25 24 23 22          1 2 3 4 5 6 7 8

Hardcover ISBN: 978-1-5064-8407-5
eBook ISBN: 978-1-5064-8408-2

Library of Congress Cataloging-in-Publication Data

Names: Kaushik, Shachi, author. | Tandon, Aishwarya, illustrator.
Title: Diwali in my new home / by Shachi Kaushik ; illustrated by Aishwarya Tandon.
Description: Minneapolis, MN : Beaming Books, 2022. | Audience: Ages 5-8. |
 Summary: "When Priya moves from India to America, she finds a way to
 share her favorite holiday with her new neighbors"-- Provided by publisher.
Identifiers: LCCN 2021058107 (print) | LCCN 2021058108 (ebook) | ISBN
 9781506484075 (hardcover) | ISBN 9781506484082 (ebook)
Subjects: CYAC: Divali--Fiction. | Neighbors--Fiction. |
 Immigrants--Fiction. | LCGFT: Picture books.
Classification: LCC PZ7.1.K3825 Di 2022  (print) | LCC PZ7.1.K3825  (ebook)
 | DDC [E]--dc23
LC record available at https://lccn.loc.gov/2021058107
LC ebook record available at https://lccn.loc.gov/2021058108

VN0004589; 9781506484075; JUL2022

Beaming Books
PO Box 1209
Minneapolis, MN 55440-1209
Beamingbooks.com

Today is Diwali, the festival of lights.
It's Priya's favorite holiday.

The colorful decorations, shimmering fireworks, and gathering
of family and friends always fill her heart with joy.

But this Diwali is quiet.

Priya is almost nine thousand miles away from India.

Here, the streets are empty, and nothing is decorated. Everything looks dull.

Priya holds back her tears, remembering her school in India.
A week before Diwali, her old school was decorated. Everyone
wore traditional outfits, made cards, and sang festive songs.

Here, no one seems to know about Diwali.

When Priya returns home this afternoon, the scents of cardamom and warm ghee greet her. The sweet aromas wrap around Priya like a hug.

"It smells like Diwali," Priya says.

She remembers her grandmother's words: "Goddess Lakshmi always visits a clean and decorated house."

Priya helps her mommy vacuum every room,
wishing for Goddess Lakshmi to come to their new home.

On the front steps, Priya sits with the colorful sand to make a flower as a rangoli—just the way she would in India.

*A rangoli will bring luck and happiness.*

The aromas floating from the kitchen window,
and the eye-catching rangoli, draw the neighbors.

"What smells delicious?"

"Wow! That looks beautiful."

"Is it something special today?"

"Yes, it's Diwali. A festival of
lights, feasts, and fireworks,"
replies Priya.

"Can we help?"

The vibrant colors in the rangoli
make the entrance glow.

Next, Priya helps her papa with the lights.

"On a new moon night, the twinkling lights will make the house bright," she says.

"Are you getting ready for Christmas already?"

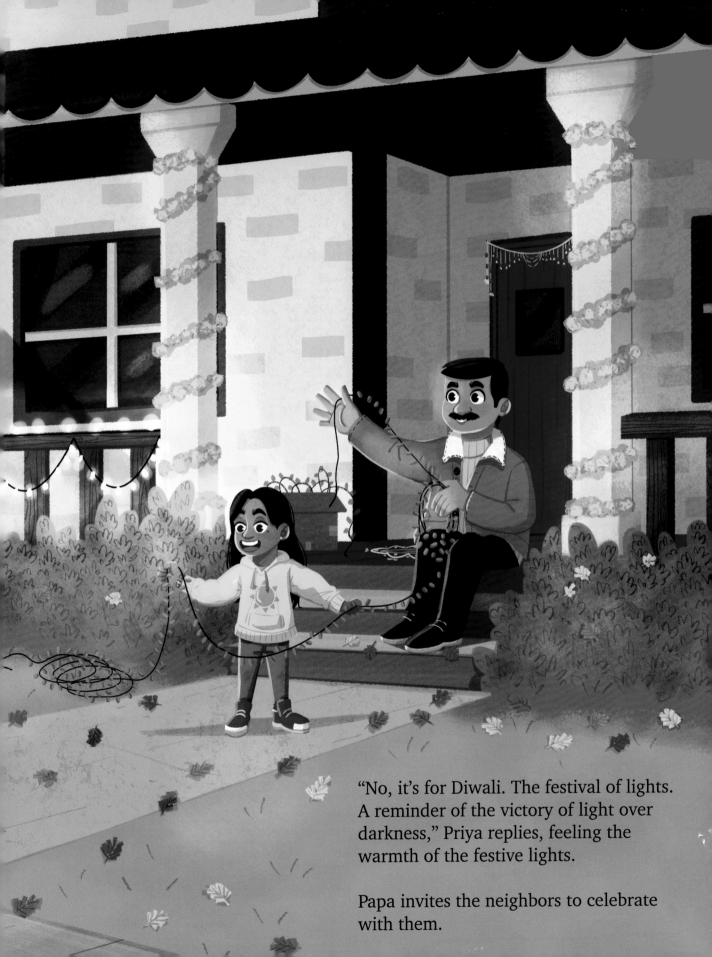

"No, it's for Diwali. The festival of lights. A reminder of the victory of light over darkness," Priya replies, feeling the warmth of the festive lights.

Papa invites the neighbors to celebrate with them.

At sunset, it's time for prayer, the puja. Priya puts on her special embroidered salwar kameez and clinks her bangles.

Seeing Mommy in a sari and Papa in a kurta pajama, she softly says, "Just like we dressed in India."

Together, they light clay lamps, the diyas, and the incense sticks in front of the deities Ganesha, Lakshmi, Rama, Sita, and Lakshman. Priya clears her throat and sings while offering marigold flowers to the gods and goddesses.

The house is filled with the smell of sandalwood incense, and with neighbors' warm smiles.

For the first time, loud giggles echo in Priya's new home.

Hope blooms inside her.

"It feels like Diwali."

And then it's time for Priya's favorite part—fireworks!

There are no sky shooters or air rockets.

But there are sparklers for everyone.

*This Diwali isn't the same as in India,
but it's Diwali in my new home.*

"Happy Diwali!"

# About Diwali

Diwali, the festival of lights, is celebrated to honor Lord Rama. Lord Rama is one of the avatars (reincarnations) of the Hindu god Vishnu and the king of the Ayodhya (pronounced Aa-yoo-dha-ya). Diwali occurs in either October or November. The date changes each year as it falls on a new-moon night.

Diwali is celebrated on the third day of the five-day festival. On this day, Lord Rama, along with his wife, Sita, and his brother, Lakshman, came back to his kingdom, Ayodhya, after spending fourteen years in exile.

To welcome their long-awaited return, everyone decorates their houses and lights lamps. Diwali celebrates the victory of light over darkness, good over evil, and hope over despair.

During Diwali, the goddess Lakshmi, who symbolizes wealth, happiness, and prosperity, is also worshipped with great devotion. It is believed that on this day, she enters houses that are clean and bright.

Because India is a diverse nation, Diwali is celebrated in different ways. In the north of India, Hindus celebrate Diwali to honor the return of Lord Rama, Lakshman, and Sita to their kingdom. People light diyas and set off fireworks. In southern India, people honor Lord Krishna, another avatar of Vishnu. On the day before Diwali, called Naraka Chaturdashi, people take an oil bath, and instead of a colorful rangoli, they draw a floor pattern called kolam with rice flour.

In America, the Association of Indians in America and other Indian organizations host events for Diwali. Most cities have Diwali Mela on the weekend after Diwali.